T0148586

Princess New Life

ZOE RUIZ

BALBOA.PRESS

A DIVISION OF HAY HOUSE

Balboa Press books may be ordered through booksellers or by contacting:

Balboa Press
A Division of Hay House
1663 Liberty Drive
Bloomington, IN 47403
www.balboapress.com.au
1 (877) 407-4847

Because of the dynamic nature of the Internet, any web addresses or
links contained in this book may have changed since publication and
may no longer be valid. The views expressed in this work are solely those
of the author and do not necessarily reflect the views of the publisher,
and the publisher hereby disclaims any responsibility for them.

The author of this book does not dispense medical advice or prescribe
the use of any technique as a form of treatment for physical, emotional,
or medical problems without the advice of a physician, either directly
or indirectly. The intent of the author is only to offer information
of a general nature to help you in your quest for emotional and
spiritual well-being. In the event you use any of the information in
this book for yourself, which is your constitutional right, the author
and the publisher assume no responsibility for your actions.

Any people depicted in stock imagery provided by Getty Images are
models, and such images are being used for illustrative purposes only.
Certain stock imagery © Getty Images.

Print information available on the last page.

ISBN: 978-1-5043-2155-6 (sc)
ISBN: 978-1-5043-2154-9 (e)

Balboa Press rev. date: 04/29/2020

*D*edicated to my eternally loved
and cherished mummy Edel.
May you be free to dance and sing in
the heavens above with your family.

Once upon a time there was a girl named Rose, she lived on a tropical island where the fish played in the ocean, the birds sang in the trees, and the palms danced in the sky. One day Rose was working in the clothing store when a Prince from a far far away island walked up to her and gave her a flower. The Prince instantly fell in love with Rose's beauty. She was the most beautiful girl on the island. Her big smile radiated and blessed everyone who was lucky enough to be in her presence. Her long thick dark hair shimmered and danced as she moved. She was the picture of perfection in her navy blue dress, red lips and high heels.

Rose's friends at work were impressed and charmed by the Prince. They all wished the prince had eyes for them, but he only had eyes for Rose. Rose's family were also charmed by the Prince. His rich, glistening robe and his white sparkling skin won over everyone on the island. But Rose didn't fall in love with the Prince, Rose felt uneasy around him. She could feel something wasn't right. She saw glimpses of darkness around him when no one was watching them.

Rose was already in love with another islander boy she knew. He was poor like Rose and had a simple life like her. No one knew of her love for this boy, only Rose. Rose didn't love the Prince, she didn't even like him, but she told no one.

Rose's family and friends saw the promise of money, a better life for them and Rose, if Rose followed the Prince. Rose obeyed her family as she was a dutiful daughter. She had served two years in the military at school which made her very respectful and dutiful to her family.

One balmy November night on the island, the Prince made love to Rose, this was the first time for Rose. On this night Rose conceived her first baby. Two months later the Prince asked for Rose to be his wife. In March, Rose walked up the palm lined street, into the church and married the Prince. The islanders cheered for joy! Rose felt she was doing the right thing and was happy.

Rose said her goodbyes to her family and friends with tears streaming down her face, but she was hopeful for her new future with her Prince. Rose boarded her Prince's ship and they set sail to his homeland, far far away.

Rose stood on the ships deck and watched her homeland become smaller and smaller in the distance until it disappeared. A great sadness and loneliness came over her. As the sun began to set, and the sky became darker, big black clouds started to form above. The wind started to blow so hard and fiercely that it threw Rose onto the floor and tore at her hair. Rain started to pour down that was cold and piercing on Rose's skin. The sky roared with thunder and cracked with lightening terrifying Rose. A dark spirit had come over her, over powering her. Her eyes were wide with terror, filled with tears, her lips trembled with fear, her voice disappeared in shock.

The Prince suddenly appeared onto the ships deck, he saw Rose in all her vulnerability, terror and despair. He slowly removed his white, shiny, rich cloak to reveal his grotesque body, his repulsive large belly. His real identity was revealed, the Prince was a Troll. Rose realised she had been tricked, but it was too late. She was trapped.

The Troll treated Rose as if she were his slave. Rose lost all her vibrance, joy, happiness, confidence, self-esteem, her voice and soon became withdrawn, depressed, bitter, angry, confused, anxious, scared and timid. As the days passed, Rose's baby grew with this darkness inside her. When her baby girl was born, she named her Princess Darkness.

The Troll, Rose and Princess Darkness lived in a small house in the city. The Troll continued to treat Rose as if she were his slave. When the Troll went away on his ship, Rose had peace and quiet. She found some other ladies from her home island and made friends with them. They sang and danced and ate just like they did on their tropical island far far away. Rose found some happiness and joy again and the dark clouds lifted until the Troll returned again.

Rose was due for her second baby. Rose's new friends could see the dark clouds around Rose and did their best to make her happy with food, dancing and singing. She had found some sweetness in life again. Rose called her second baby girl Princess Sweetness.

The Troll continued to go away on his ship and come back to Rose and the two baby girls. His evil dark spirit bought tears, pain and torment to Rose and the two babies every time he returned.

Rose was due to have her third baby. She tried escaping with the two babies, running away from the Troll through the dark, scary streets. She was hopeful she could escape one day, but the Troll kept finding her. When her third girl was born, she named her Princess New Life. Hoping for a new life and better days. When Princess New Life was 7 years old she knew of the dark scary storms and how her much her mum was miserable. This made Princess New Life very upset. She told her mum whilst standing in front of her dressing table mirror brushing her hair that she needed to leave the Troll. Rose listened to Princess New Life but said nothing.

The Troll grew angry and frustrated of Rose's repeated attempts of running away. One day, he took Rose and the three girls up a long long windy road, up a big mountain, then along a dry, hot road until finally he stopped at the bottom of a big hill in the middle of nowhere. Rose and the three girls were surrounded by long, brown, spindly grass, brown termite mounds and brown rocks. There the Troll had a brown and yellow tin shed where Rose and the three girls lived with the Troll. The Troll continued to go away on his ship and return with the same darkness, the same storms.

None of Rose's friends knew where Rose went, she just disappeared one day. No one visited Rose and Rose didn't find any new friends.

One day the Troll came back from the sea, and he bought with him a darker, heavier, more aggressive and scarier storm. That night Rose was tortured like no other night she had experienced, it was the worst storm that drew lots of blood, that blackened her body from head to toe. The three Princesses were petrified that night too, Princess Darkness hid in the black shadows, too scared and numb to speak

or move. Princess Sweetness cried under her blanket and cried herself to sleep. Princess New Life was tortured inside seeing her mum being tortured by the storm, finally she screamed and roared for the storm to stop, she screamed so loud, so clearly that finally the storm stopped. There was silence and stillness. The night passed, the sun rose and the Princesses went to school.

Later that morning Rose went to the Princesses school, she covered her body from head to toe with clothing wearing big sunglasses so that only glimpses of her black and purple face showed. Tears streamed down her face, her lips trembled. No words were spoken, the Princesses teachers and Princesses understood. The Princesses quickly and quietly packed their backpacks and fled to the next town with their mum. The Troll burned the long spindly brown grass on that hill and all of Rose's beloved cats were tied to trees and burned too.

The new town had lush green rolling hills, green grass, pretty colourful flowers, rainbows and birds singing in the trees. Rose and the three Princesses made lots of new friends and they sang, danced, laughed and ate together. They were filled with lightness, joy and love for the first time. The girls grew taller and Rose was loved and felt loved.

One day while the girls were playing there came a knock on the door. Princess Darkness opened the door and there stood the Troll, wearing his most charming, rich cloak. He charmed all of Roses friends who embraced him with open arms. The Troll reminded Rose of her duties to him and she dutifully returned to the brown and yellow shed, at the bottom of that brown hill, surrounded by brown rocks, brown termite mounds and long brown spindly grass.

Not long after Rose and the Princesses returned to the shed, the storms started again, however they were milder, and more tolerable by Rose. Rose always worked hard cleaning houses, working at restaurants and cafes waitressing and cleaning, working at the fruit and vegetable markets, and working on strawberry, mango, avocado and herb farms. Once Rose and Princess New Life worked on a longan farm together which they enjoyed and laughed together. Rose struggled to keep up

at the longan farm and Princess New Life helped her keep up with the other farm workers. No matter how hard Rose worked she struggled to buy food for her Princesses as the Troll never helped her. Rose was always too thin and exhausted from working long hours and raising her Princesses. The years went on and not one of Rose's friends visited her in that isolated, hidden shed, no one could find her or contact her. There was no more singing, dancing, laughing or eating.

As the years passed and the Princesses grew older, the storms continued and left permanent black scars on Roses heart and mind. Her heart and mind grew dark and her darkness spread to her Princesses, now Rose bought her own storms.

Princess Darkness left home to peruse her own life, then Princess Sweetness. Princess New Life knew she had to get away from her mum's dark storms, so she packed her bags and left the brown and yellow shed in her final year of school. Rose stayed in the brown and yellow shed going about her duties for the Troll. The Troll continued to bring dark storms to Rose, but only Rose knew of these storms and what happened.

As the years rolled on, the Princesses avoided the Troll and encouraged Rose to do the same and run away again to have happiness, joy, rainbows and sunshine in her life again. Rose was lost and confused, her clarity and self-confidence had disappeared. The years of dark storms had scarred her mind, heart and spirit forever. She felt trapped and obligated at the same time. She was torn and conflicted inside and was weaker, and grew weaker and more defeated as the days passed.

Princess New Life saw her mum's pain and tried many times to set her free from her slavery the Troll bought her. But Rose never took the key of freedom from Princess New Life. Princess New Life was distraught and cried every time her mum never took the freedom key, eventually Princess New Life gave up trying to set her mum free.

Rose saw the photos and heard the stories of Princess New Life's worldly travels and adventures. Rose treasured all the gifts she was given from her Princess's travels, and secretly wished she was with her travelling the world. She wished she saw all those beautiful places too. Rose had a world globe by her bed and dreamed of what travelling must be like for Princess New Life. She fantasised and dreamed as she looked at Princess New Life's photos over and over again to the wee hours of the night. Rose cut pretty pictures out from books and magazines and stuck them on the walls in her room

to make it more beautiful. She passed her time gardening, making the most of the chaotic, rubbish laden, brown dry grounds around her that was filled with snakes. She reflected on her life, remembering her childhood memories, remembering her family back on the tropical island, far far away. She was lonely and very sad. The Troll went back to Rose's tropical island many times and never took Rose. He bought two

homes there, one in the city, the other at the top of a skyscraper. There he enjoyed Rose's homeland, her culture, her people, her food in the company of another islander lady he tried to keep a secret. This greatly depressed and angered Rose. It scarred her already heavy bleeding heart even more, with thick black lashes that seeped red and black.

The Troll bought more homes in the city where Rose first made new friends, however he didn't let Rose stay in that city. He kept her isolated, alone, in the unfinished brown and yellow shed. Rose was surrounded by vermin at the brown and yellow shed at the bottom of that hill where rats, snakes, spiders, entangled by weeds and thorns grew. The rats, snakes and spiders entered the shed at night, into Rose's room and scared her at night. She did the best to protect herself from these and made the most of her cage.

Princess New Life often visited and took Rose out for special delightful meals, cakes, coffee and treats. Princess New Life spoiled Rose as she knew the Troll never did. She bought her pretty flowers, blankets, pillows, tea cups, manicures and massages. They spent time together by beautiful dams with water fountains, amongst pretty peacocks and talked to the lamas, goats, cows and chickens.

Princess New Life had Roses love of dancing. Princess New Life was dancing with her fairy friends under a mushroom when one day a friend told her of the dark clouds that covered the mushroom and engulfed a number of fairies who were Princess New Life's friends.

Princess New Life remembered the pain, tears and images of the dark storms from her childhood. She felt so much sadness, weakness and anger all at the same time. A black panther told her one day when she was walking in the forest to take her fairy friends and lead them to sunshine, rainbows and flowers, away from the darkness at the mushroom. The black panther knew the fire and power hidden deep down inside Princess New Life, he could see the flames flickering in her eyes. Princess New Life thanked the

black panther and did what he told her to do. She saved her fairy friends from the dark storms over that mushroom, and bought sunshine to many others hidden in other dark mushrooms whom she didn't know.

Princess New Life missed her mum so much, one day, she decided she would try again to take her on a holiday. She tried a few years earlier but Rose didn't go. Princess New Life was hopeful. Princess New Life's dreams came true and Rose went on the holiday to see Princess Sweetness and her baby cubs.

They all had a beautiful holiday together, walking along the river, across bridges, hopping from stone to stone, sitting under orange, red and purple Autumn leaves, feeding birds, chasing rabbits, playing games with the baby cubs, eating pizza on the grass, walking on the sand at the beach, building sandcastles, walking over soft seaweed that squished between their toes, listening to the ocean waves crashing and feeling the wind blowing through their long black hair. It was such a sweet time of love and connection that Princess New Life had wished for years, and so did Rose

secretly. The ocean reminded Rose of her homeland and family, it reminded her of the deep, dark loneliness she felt inside that she hid from the world, even herself. Rose told Princess New Life while on holidays with the biggest smile on her face, 'This is living!'. This bought so much joy to Princess New Life, to see Rose filled with sunshine again she hadn't seen in decades. Rose was radiating with happiness, she stood tall, walked confidently, flicking her long thick shiny black hair in the sun, her chin and heart pointing up towards the sun. Rose told Princess New Life secretly as they walked

together counting the rabbits they saw, 'I'm free, no Troll, I can do what I want!'. And with that, Rose whipped out of her jacket a giant chocolate bar and started eating it for breakfast. Princess New Life was sad and delighted to see and hear Rose say this, she chuckled inside at the size of the chocolate bar.

Whilst on holidays the family fell ill, they broke out with fever, sneezing and coughing. Princess New Life bounced back fast and cooked healthy food and gave medicine to the family, especially to Rose. Rose called Princess New Life her nurse. Even in their ill health they laughed and ate together.

It was time to take Rose back to the brown and yellow shed. Princess New Life didn't want to take her but she knew she had no choice. The Troll was already calling Princess Sweetness asking for her return. Rose was torn inside, at Princess New Life's home she was surrounded by beautiful manicured gardens, pretty plants and flowers, an immaculate home of perfect furniture, decorations and pictures on the walls, fresh ocean breezes, green grass and swaying palms in the wind. This was just the kind of home Rose dreamed of, she remembered

encouraging Princess new Life to move here almost 4 years ago. Rose knew her duties and reluctantly went back to the brown and yellow shed. She saw the Troll and slumped into a chair. She felt and looked defeated. So did Princess New Life, she ached inside. Seeing the Troll repulsed her as well as the unsightly shed and rubbish. She hastily left feeling unsettled inside that Saturday afternoon. The Troll was bellowing nonsense that afternoon, he was always bellowing nonsense that was meaningless to Rose and Princess New Life.

Three days later on Tuesday the Troll left on his ship. On Thursday, two days later Rose set herself free from the Trolls cage of 39 years. Her soul longed to be with her sisters, mum and dad. The whispers from the ocean that day whilst on holidays called her soul so strongly, she didn't want to be lonely anymore. She got to feel sunshine, rainbows and joy again being with her Princesses and baby cubs on that

holiday. She didn't want to feel that isolation again. She didn't want to feel trapped with the Troll anymore and go through anymore dark storms. Her heart, mind and spirit were scarred so deeply, so many times, she didn't want to bear anymore scars. She set herself free peacefully in her sleep, without the darkness of the Troll around her.

Rose transformed into a cocoon and then into a brilliant big blue butterfly. Princess New Life felt severe neck pain and head pressure on the Thursday Rose passed, she also struggled to breath easily and her heart raced. She bought six navy blue dresses on Saturday night and was told by the old wise owl in the tree to go to the magical secret gardens. She did three times the following day, Sunday, and watched the blue butterflies fly high up and around and around. She was compelled to wear blue on Tuesday. No one had heard from Rose for over a week. Princess Sweetness from far away called the caring bears to check on Rose.

Princess Sweetness called Princess New Life Wednesday afternoon and told her Rose had died. Princess New Life roared like a tiger, the fire deep in her exploded like a volcano erupting and burning everything around her. Her grief, anger and sadness tore her heart and spirit into a million pieces. She travelled to hell and back that night. She went to the brown and yellow shed with her friends the Swan

and Elephant. She saw Roses blood on the pillow and mattress. She took some of her mum's cherished belongings and kept them by her bed. Thursday the next morning there was a huge brown butterfly on the pot plant by Princess New Life's bedroom. Its wings were torn and uneven. It was majestic in all its imperfections. It stayed by Princess New Life's bedroom all day.

On Sunday, Mother's Day, the Troll and Princess Sweetness had cleaned out Rose's room of her belongings, they were strewn all over the dirt. When Princess New Life saw her mums cherished items on the dirt, she roared like a tiger. The sound shook the brown and yellow shed, scared the Troll and startled Princess Sweetheart. The Troll kept out of Princess New Life's way as she went through Rose's precious belongings looking to save what she

could. She pulled everything out that was already packed to be taken away. She left that day with the precious gifts Princess New Life had given Rose over the years, and other personal items of Roses. Princess New Life could feel Rose's anger inside her when she saw how her precious belongings were being treated. Her body had yet to be taken to the Sacred Valley. Princess New Life left the Troll and the shed, burning quietly inside.

That night a dancing cat who she had met one night invited her to his tree house that night. Princess New Life was fed, nurtured, nourished and humoured by the dancing cat and his smiling friends. As she walked out of the tree house, she saw two blue butterfly pictures leaning on the wall. She burst into tears. The dancing cat gave the pictures to Princess New Life, as she left, she whispered to the dancing cat, 'You're the kind of cat mum wanted to marry'.

Rose sent butterflies, stories and messages to Princess New Life intensely all week. The Troll tried to taunt her the night before Rose's body was taken to the Sacred Valley, but she was too empowered with Rose's messages. On Friday at the Sacred Valley, Princess New Life delivered the speech of her life. She could see the darkness hovering to her left, the

Troll, Princess Darkness and the Trolls family and friends. And the light to her right, Princess Sweetness and her cubs, Princess New Life's friends, and friends who left the far far away tropical island years ago just like Rose. Rose told Princess New Lift what to say in her speech, and she did it perfectly. There was not one heart that was left un-weeping.

The Troll and Princess Darkness never said goodbye to Princess New Life. Princess New Life understands the blue butterflies are Rose's spirit. She understands why. She understands the perfection and accepts what is. She has peace. The wise old owl told Princess New Life that Rose had forgiven the Troll and that she must now too. Princess New Life climbed to the top of the blue mountain and forgave the Troll.

The Troll is forever tormented and punished. Princess Darkness and Princess Sweetheart have inner turmoil and confusion with some moments of peace. The Troll two days after the Sacred Valley, went on this ship to see his secret second family, his islander lady and her family.

Many moons later, the Troll was out on his ship when he fell off the ship and into the ocean. The ocean took him down to the depths of the sea where he was set free of his dark spirit. He now has peace; he has been set free. The next day the ship was surrounded by turtles. The Troll hides his torment, punishment and guilt in a huge hump on his back protected by a thick, hard shell.

Princess New Life continues to garden, her garden is bigger and more beautiful now with lots of colourful roses. She visits the magical secret gardens regularly. Now when she sees a blue butterfly, she sees a purple dragonfly as well. Rose has found her old love sweetheart and reunited. They dance and play happily.

Princess New Life often goes to the ocean to write, she sometimes sees a turtle sitting on the sand next to a goanna, he has finally found a soul mate and the goanna loves him unconditionally.

Princess New Life continues to use her fire inside for good, she makes Rose proud every day. She continues to provide sunshine, rainbows and flowers for women to dance and free themselves. She continues to roar like a tiger. She continues to travel the world and see butterflies near her. She often scratches their bellies. She married the black panther in a perfect garden filled with blue butterflies and together they had baby cubs full of fire and passion, and the souls of Princess New Life's mum, and the black panther's dad and granddad live on.

As the years went on, Princess Sweetness and Princess Darkness found more sunshine and peace.

And they all lived happily ever after.

The End.

Printed in the United States
By Bookmasters